FANTASTIC
TALES OF
DRAGONS

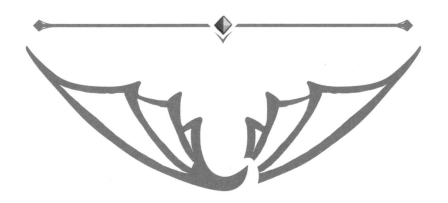

Contents

About the Authors

Helen H. Wu

Helen H. Wu is a children's book author and illustrator, as well as a translator and publisher. She is the author of *Tofu Takes Time* and *Long Goes to Dragon School*. Fascinated by the differences and similarities between cultures, Helen shares stories that empower children to understand the world and our connections. Helen lives in San Diego, California, with her family and two children.

Renata Piątkowska

Renata Piątkowska is one of the best-known and loved Polish children's book authors. She has won many literary prizes and several of her books have been translated into other languages. She has also had her work turned into films and plays. Her stories are packed with humour, wordplay and lots of fun!

Naibe Reynoso

Naibe Reynoso is a Mexican-American multi-Emmy® award-winning journalist and author based in Los Angeles, California. She is the founder of Con Todo Press, an award-winning publishing house that creates books to amplify the stories and voices of underrepresented communities. Naibe is also a board member for the Mexican-American Cultural Foundation and was recently named a Latina of Influence by *Hispanic Lifestyle.*

Nnedi Okorafor

Nnedi Okorafor is an award-winning *New York Times* bestselling novelist of science fiction and fantasy stories for children, young adults and adults. Born in the United States to Nigerian immigrant parents, Nnedi is known for drawing from African cultures to create captivating tales with unforgettable characters. She lives in Phoenix, Arizona, with her daughter, Anyaugo.

Meet Aiden

Hi, my name's Aiden and I'm a dragon.
Build me and then read all about me
and my awesome ancestors.

Build Your Dragon

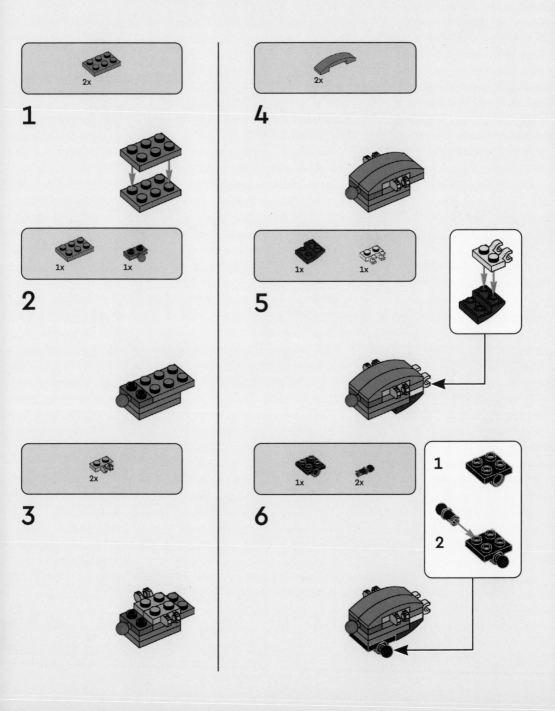

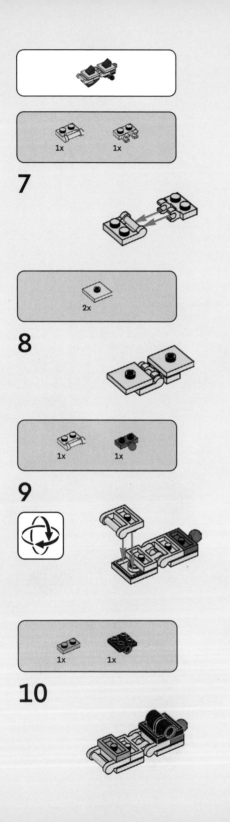

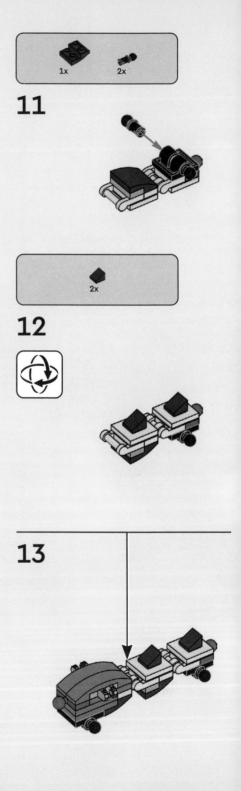

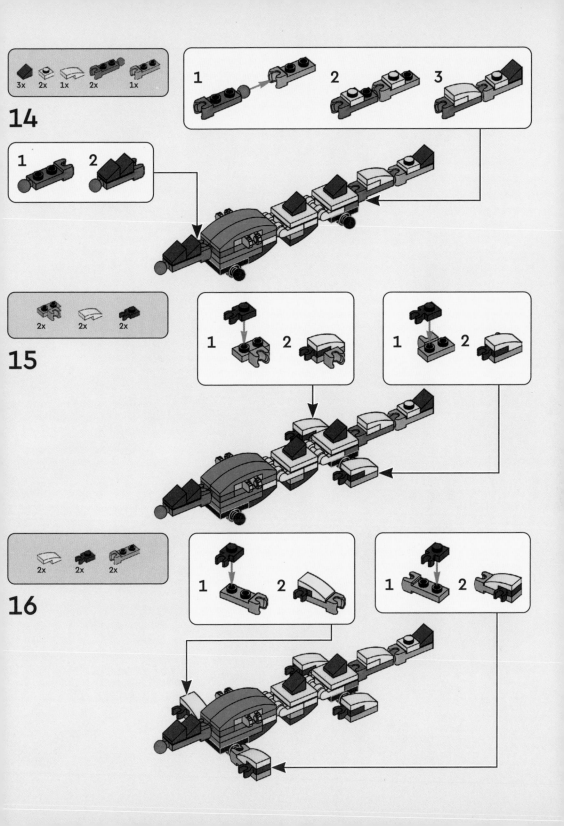

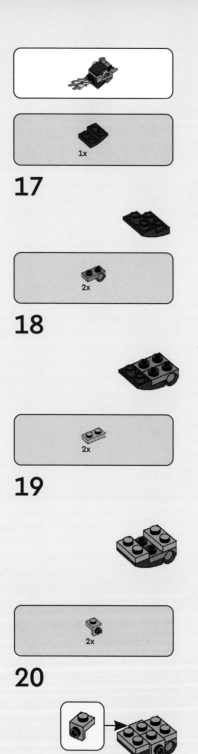

17

18

19

20

21

22

23

24

25

2x **2x**

2x

26

2x

27

2x

28

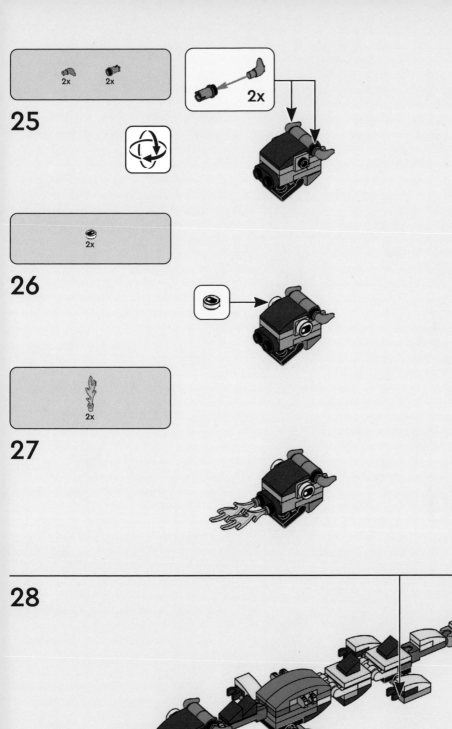

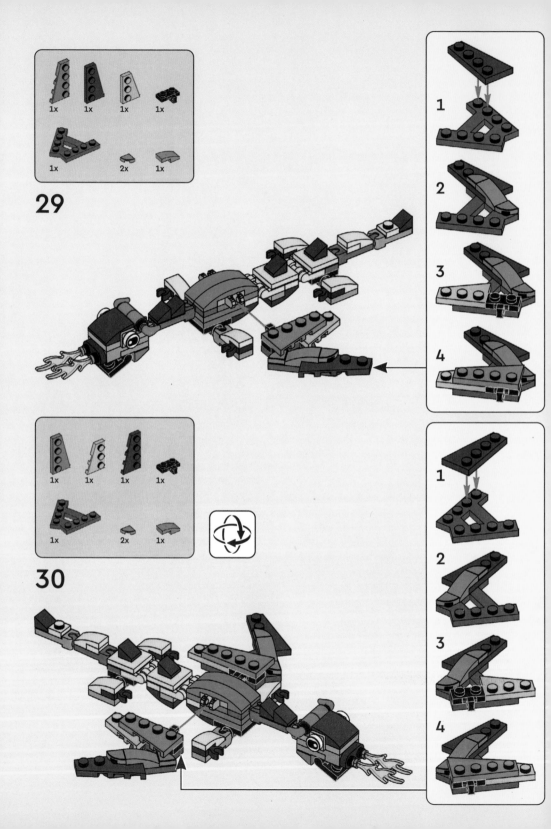

List of Pieces

2x
6168634

1x
4161329

2x
6329648

2x
6374192

2x
6338180

5x
6029947

2x
302424

2x
6147010

2x
6126050

2x
6337231

2x
4501232

2x
6266244

1x
4225201

4x
6344752

1x
6000071

2x
6021539

3x
302128

2x
6249427

4x
6240467

3x
4164037

1x
4502091

1x
4529954

5x
4504375

3x
6255896

2x
6360075

1x
6223171

2x
6167741

1x
6020145

1x
6020146

4x
6337003

1x
6248944

3x
6043656

3x
6043639

2x
6039479

2x
6039482

4161329

4160866

6368619

6378120

281726

Aiden the Mosaic Dragon

Aiden was having one of those days. He spilled his cocoa when his wing knocked over his mug. Then he bumped his horn on the ceiling and tripped over the rug, which made his golden scales clank against the floor as he fell. THUD. Aiden let out a sigh of relief, which ended up setting fire to his bookcase.

He quickly took his fire extinguisher and put the flames out. Aiden was always prepared for an accident, as he couldn't control his fire-breathing like other dragons could. Not that he knew many other dragons. In fact, Aiden didn't really know any other dragons at all, apart from his grandmother. He mainly knew people, and they showed him how to use useful things like fire extinguishers.

Aiden removed the books to check the damage to the bookcase. Then, reaching over to clean up the cocoa, Aiden slipped. He steadied himself, but his golden tail smacked against the wall as he regained his balance. Luckily, Aiden lived in the basement of a building called Long Meadow, so his neighbours hardly ever heard him.

As he arranged his books again, Aiden spotted one that his grandmother had given him for his birthday. Opening the heavy cover, he saw the message she had written inside it: *Be proud of who you are, my golden boy.*

Looking in the mirror at his lizard-like face and rainbow-coloured wings, Aiden didn't see a "golden boy". Sure, he had golden scales, but he felt like he so often did: just a bit weird and different. He didn't look like his neighbours or even his grandmother. Dragons were usually one colour, but gazing at himself in the mirror, Aiden just saw ... a mess.

Aiden felt like going back to bed and hiding under the covers. But maybe today was a good day to finally

read his new book. It would at least keep him out of trouble, since he was having "one of those days". Maybe reading the book would feel like being with his grandmother. She was always Aiden's biggest champion and helped him to see the good side of things.

So, Aiden made another mug of cocoa and opened the heavy cover of the book. As he read the introduction, he realized grandma hadn't bought the book ... she'd made it!

These stories are the legends of your ancestors from all around the world. They tell the stories of the extraordinary dragons you are descended from.

Let's begin with Yinglong, a golden dragon from China who had a special relationship with humans, just like you ...

The Legend of Yinglong

By Helen H. Wu

Once upon a time in ancient China, there lived a kind dragon named Yinglong, or Responsive Dragon. She was called Responsive Dragon because if the people cried out to her for more or less rain, she would have mercy and respond to their pleas. Yinglong and her helping heart had been there since the very beginning of time. She flew in the sky with her long, shiny tail dancing through dewy clouds, and brought gentle rains with her invisible wings, helping plants and life to grow. Yinglong also helped the mother goddess, Nüwa, create humans. She sprinkled raindrops and turned dust into clay, which Nüwa used to mould the first people. Ever since then, Yinglong had been enchanted by humans, watching them from afar and looking after them.

Hundreds of years later, on the Yellow River plain, the Yellow Emperor ruled his tribes with wisdom and kindness. He invented carts and boats and taught his people how to dredge waterways and build dams. The Yellow Emperor was grateful to Yinglong for bringing timely rains so the crops could thrive. Yinglong cherished the Emperor for his kindness, and always offered her help.

But soon, a dark power began to rise. One day, when Yinglong was roaming the skies, she saw an evil man named Chiyou, who declared himself the ruler of the land. He was very strong and vicious. His body was powerful and his hands wielded terrible axes. He had eighty-one brothers, who were the rulers of eighty-one clans. Chiyou and his brothers forged and assembled sharp spears and swords to control their people through fear. Chiyou spent all his time training his forces instead of caring for crops or building dams like the Yellow Emperor had done. His men grew stronger, but the land was left unattended.

Yinglong saw the ruthless acts of Chiyou and his brothers. "They value power more than kindness," Yinglong scowled. "Chiyou needs to be taught a lesson."

Yinglong turned her invisible wings into huge gloomy clouds that brought howling wind and pouring rains, with crashing thunder and flashing lightning. Yinglong thought that if Chiyou saw the storm coming, he would stop his ruthless ways and turn back to care for the land and people instead. But the land hadn't been worked on for such a long time that the heavy rains flooded the fields.

"Master, we don't have enough food," one of Chiyou's brothers complained. "Maybe we can borrow some from the Yellow Emperor for the winter."

Chiyou scoffed at the suggestion.

"I have a better idea," Chiyou declared to the clans. "We will conquer the Yellow Emperor's people and take their lands."

They all hooted and cheered, raising their spears and beating them against their shields. The deafening sound made Chiyou feel invincible.

Gasping at what she saw, Yinglong retreated back to the skies. "Oh no! Have I caused chaos?" She wished she had never used her power to bring the storms.

When the Yellow Emperor heard about Chiyou, he called to his elders for advice.

"We should negotiate," one of the elders said.

A few murmured their agreement, until an elder general stood up and all of them went quiet.

"Chiyou is a ruthless man that destroys everything in his way," he said. "We cannot reason with him."

Slowly, the Yellow Emperor stood. "I know battles are not our calling, but I must defend those that are under my protection."

Yinglong was moved by the Yellow Emperor's bravery. "I should help more. But how?" she thought to herself, scratching her horns. "After all, this conflict is my fault."

The Yellow Emperor bravely led his people into the battlefield at Zhuolu.

"Surrender before I crush you!" Chiyou yelled.

"Your greed will lead you to your doom," the Yellow Emperor warned his foe with steely resolve.

The battle began. The sound of steel upon steel and man versus man made the ground tremble.

Yinglong watched the exchange from the clouds. She felt uncomfortable watching the battle, but she wasn't sure how to stop it. She felt powerless and small.

The Yellow Emperor didn't have strong spears and swords like Chiyou's warriors. But the Yellow Emperor's people were courageous and they fought with great strategy. Angered by the battle being more evenly matched than he expected, Chiyou howled, "Let's cloud their vision!"

A group of Chiyou's men came over with huge, fan-like machines that had blades propped up on wooden frames. As they spun a lever, the machines created a sandstorm. The Yellow Emperor's people became unable to see either in front or behind, and were trapped.

Yinglong felt the sorrow in the Yellow Emperor's heart. She did not want him to lose his country and his people to such a brute. "I wish I could help," Yinglong confessed to the Yellow Emperor as she swooped down from the clouds. "I can only bring rain, but heavy rain would flood everything and everyone ... including your people. What can I do?"

The Yellow Emperor was grateful to Yinglong. He thought for a while. "I have a plan, but I need your help," he said at last.

"I will do anything to end this conflict," Yinglong promised.

During the night, the Yellow Emperor commanded his people to build dams with rocks and wood. They dug trenches for the water to flow. They built dykes to protect their carts and equipment. They moved the people to the highlands. Meanwhile, the Yellow Emperor built stairs.

The next morning, when Chiyou's fighters eagerly sounded their horns to re-start the battle, the Yellow Emperor went to the top of the stairs and climbed on Yinglong's back.

Yinglong took to the sky and flew over the Yellow Emperor's people. When the people saw their leader on the dragon's back, it renewed their hope.

Chiyou told his men to use the sandstorm machines once more, but Yinglong knew what she needed to do.

With a fierce growl, she expanded her usually invisible wings into thick rainclouds. Thunder crackled and rain pelted down, defeating the sandstorm. Spears and swords were useless against the storm. Chiyou's fighters battled to hold their ground, but to no avail. They tried to pile stones to keep the water away, but they weren't fast enough, and their stone piles soon collapsed. The Yellow Emperor's men fought courageously and regained their terrain.

"Hold on tight," Yinglong warned the Yellow Emperor. As she felt him gripping tight, Yinglong went into a freefall toward the ground.

"You will crash!" Chiyou called out. But Yinglong raised herself up at the last minute and struck at the earth with her powerful long tail. The earth burst open and Chiyou's fighters were pulled into a wild torrent of water.

Finally, Yinglong landed before Chiyou.

"It's over," said the Yellow Emperor as he climbed down from Chiyou's back. "Surrender and I will spare your people."

Chiyou and his army were no match for the joint forces of the Emperor and the dragon.

Chiyou roared with both fury and shame. He lifted his axe and hurled it towards the dragon, but as he did so he slipped and fell on the wet ground.

Yinglong created a flood that swept Chiyou away, never to be seen again.

The Yellow Emperor then said to Chiyou's men, "Your lives will be spared, as long as you agree to live in peace."

Some muttered their disagreement, but when one of Chiyou's elder generals stood up, all went quiet. "We pledge allegiance to kindness, wisdom and courage," said the elder general.

"Hooray!" everyone cheered.

Yinglong created more rivers that extended across the land, helping to avoid floods and also keeping the lands fertile.

"The real power is helping others," the Yellow Emperor said, paying his respects to Yinglong. With Yinglong's help, a united nation was born. From then on, the Chinese people cherished Yinglong's brave response and considered themselves to be the descendants of dragons.

Emerging from his basement, the sun reflected off Aiden's golden scales. His neighbour, Bob, was washing the building's windows. Bob lived on the floor right above Aiden. He always kept an eye on the building, making small improvements, even though it wasn't his job.

"I heard your kerfuffle downstairs, Aiden," Bob said, still washing the windows. "You okay?"

Aiden felt embarrassed and accidentally coughed out a little fire. It narrowly missed Bob but gave his neighbour's metal water bucket a short blast of heat.

"Oh dear!" Aiden blushed, feeling even more embarrassed than before, but Bob said it was just what he needed.

"The water in my bucket was cold, and I was just about to go and replace it," Bob explained. He gestured to his bucket. "But now, thanks to you, the water is warm."

As Aiden sheepishly looked down at the ground, Bob asked, "What book have you got there?"

"It's a book of dragon legends," Aiden replied. "My grandmother made it for me."

"Wonderful!" Bob said. "Does it have the story of the Responsive Dragon? That's my favourite."

"You know the story of Yinglong?" Aiden asked in surprise.

Bob laughed. "Of course! There is so much to learn from dragon legends. Yinglong is my favourite because she worked with the Yellow Emperor and his people to help their peaceful nation flourish."

Aiden thought about the mighty dragon as Bob pretended to be Chiyou, washing away in the flood. Aiden laughed so hard that he hiccupped and set another small patch of grass on fire. Bob quickly poured water over the flames.

"Sorry, Bob," Aiden said sadly.

"You may not be able to control your power for now, but you're a kind neighbour," said Bob. "Just like Yinglong, you always try to help those that need it." Bob returned to window washing and stretched up to reach the top of a window.

Aiden thought of Yinglong again, and how the Emperor had built stairs to climb on Yinglong's back. Aiden excused himself for a minute and returned with some LEGO® pieces. Instead of stairs, Aiden quickly built a stepladder for Bob.

"Impressive!" Bob said. "See? You are kind, like Yinglong. And that's what makes you wonderful."

Aiden thought about what Bob said as he settled on the grass and opened his grandmother's book to the next legend:

Dragons are the fiercest creatures of all. The Wawel Dragon tormented the people of Kraków in Poland. But as the humans in this story learn, strength alone is not enough. What you have, dear Aiden, is better than fierceness or strength. You have intellect and heart.

The Legend of
the Wawel Dragon

By Renata Piątkowska

This story happened in Poland, many, many years ago. So long ago, in fact, that even the oldest people in Kraków can't remember when it occurred. It all started by the Vistula River, which flowed lazily around the foot of a tall hill. During the day, water glittered in the sunshine, and at night, it served as a mirror for the moon who admired her reflection, while the surprised fish stared at her googly-eyed from the depths. But neither the moon nor the fish knew that something else was looking at their reflections, too – something enormous, winged, green and evil.

But first things first. By the river, on the Wawel Hill, there was a fairytale castle. It was built from shiny bricks, with defensive walls and towers that reached to the sky. It was King Krak's fortress. King Krak was a wise and just ruler, and Kraków was a wonderful place to live. The city gates were always open for merchants and craftsmen such as bakers, tailors, blacksmiths and shoemakers. Taverns served roast lamb, rainbow trout and onion flatbread, while musicians played heartily and merrily for the dancing people.

But this would all soon change. First, sheep and cows started disappearing from pastures. Then someone

described huge claw marks in the mud by the river. There was talk of demolished cottages and trees torn from the ground. Tradespeople in the market square bustled around their stalls, chattering:

"I heard a terrible beast was spotted near here."

"People say it can fly."

"It eats everything that comes its way."

"It will soon come for our sheep and cows!"

"They say it breathes fire."

"Maybe the king will know what to do about it."

Soon, it became clear that a really vicious beast had settled by the Vistula River. It wasn't like the usual troublemakers who bothered the village, such as evil spirits that caused bad smells in huts or mischievous creatures who dropped fleas into people's shirts. This was a real dragon. A huge beast with flapping wings, a lizard's tail and a fiery breath. The dragon lived by the river, in a cave under the Wawel Hill. When he crawled out of the cave at dawn, he roared so terribly that the limestone rocks shook and fell to the ground. People looked on and trembled as he spread his wings and soared across the sky.

As the beast flew, flames burst from his mouth and burned everything they touched, wreaking havoc and

creating dread. The dragon torched forests, houses and bridges. He snatched more sheep from pastures and wiped out large orchards with his tail. Fear fell on the people of Kraków. They were afraid to leave their houses, and scared children hid under their beds, whispering to each other.

"I wonder where dragons come from," said one.

"I heard they hatch from rooster eggs. And a toad sits on them for nine years on top of a dung heap!" said another.

But the dragon didn't go away. Every day, he demanded food with a roar, and if people didn't bring roast mutton to his cave, he helped himself to whatever he found on the pastures, in larders and in cellars. Shepherds jumped to their feet and ran in panic as soon as they saw him approaching. Those who had seen him shivered in their shoes at the mere mention of the flying beast with a fiery tongue.

"Things can't go on like this!" King Krak said as he pounded his fist on a table. He called a meeting of his most trusted advisors, prophets and soldiers.

For three days they debated, sighed and shook their heads. Some even tugged nervously at their moustaches. Finally, they decided to send town criers to the four corners of the world. They announced the following:

"King Krak summons brave warriors, daredevils and adventurers to defeat the Wawel Dragon. Whoever succeeds will receive a generous reward!"

The next day, daring knights began to flock to Kraków, lured by the prospect of reward and fame. In heavy armour, with swords, spears and battleaxes, they went to try their chances with the dragon. The skirmishes didn't last long. As soon as the Wawel Dragon opened his mouth, his foul-smelling breath made the knights cover their noses, faint and slip off

their horses. How can you fight an enemy that you cannot get close to? How can you fight an enemy who will scorch you from afar, or ram you into the ground with his spiky tail?

Each day more knights came, and each day the dragon dealt with them with ease. One month passed and still none of the warriors had managed to defeat the beast. Kraków citizens started to lose hope that they would ever get rid of this terrible creature.

King Krak constantly paced with worry. He couldn't eat and he couldn't sleep. He just wandered restlessly around the castle courtyard, brooding. "What will happen when the dragon gets all the sheep, cows and goats? Will he turn against us? Maybe we should flee this land that turned out to be jinxed?"

The king's gloomy thoughts were interrupted by a young man named Twiner. He was the best shoemaker in Kraków, and had often been praised for his cleverness and agility. When he appeared

before the king, he bowed. "Forgive my boldness, Your Majesty," he said. "But I would like to face the dragon, too."

"But how will you fight him?" the worried ruler asked. "Where's your armour? Your sharp sword? Your shield, spear or battleaxe? Where's your steed?"

"I don't have armour, or a horse," the shoemaker admitted. "But the dragon has already defeated so many brave warriors. They had spears, swords and battleaxes, but they didn't manage to beat the beast. I believe I can do it by means of deception, instead of force."

King Krak looked at the shoemaker with disbelief. How could this scrawny youth outsmart the dragon? The king fidgeted in his throne and sighed. "I don't know your plan, but think it through well," he said. "This beast is no laughing matter."

Twiner immediately got to work. He built a fake sheep, covered it with soft fleece, and stuffed it with a hand-sewn bag full of lumps of sulfur. He added some sticky tar, a bit of stinging hemlock and some of the poisonous flower Monkswood. Then he closed up the fake sheep with the last brick and propped it up on four strong legs. The animal looked very real. Nobody suspected it was created by the shoemaker!

In the evening, Twiner tied a cloth over his mouth to avoid smelling the odour hanging over the dragon's den. Then he put the fake sheep on a cart and headed

out. When he arrived, he tiptoed toward the cave. He looked around, placed the fake sheep in tall grass, and hid behind some nearby bushes. A moment later, the dragon's eyes lit up in the falling dusk. The hungry beast crawled out of the cave and devoured the bait with one snap of his jaws.

Twiner held his breath and waited for what was about to happen. His hands were sweaty as he watched the huge dragon blow smoke out of his nose, lick his lips and turn back to the cave.

The shoemaker hung his head. "It didn't work," he said to himself. "It was all for nothing."

Just as Twiner was giving up hope, he heard a loud roar. Everything in the area shook as the beast fiercely whipped the ground with his tail. The dragon felt burning in his throat and then in his entire body. He rushed to the river, bent his head and drank quickly. He drank and drank and drank. With each gulp, he swelled up more and more. He became bigger and wider, until suddenly he exploded with a big BANG! It sounded as if a hundred cannons had fired at once. Some of the bricks from the dragon rained down on the Kraków streets and stalls. Everybody poured into the streets, laughing and hugging because they knew where the bricks had come from. Finally, they could breathe a sigh of relief. The dragon was defeated.

Twiner was the happiest of them all. The cheering crowds carried him to King Krak, who greeted the shoemaker with open arms.

"I promised you a generous reward and I will keep my word," King Krak said.

He gave the brave young man a chest full of gold and gems and awarded him the title of the Bravest Knight in Kraków.

This story happened a long time ago. Since then, the city has grown and become more beautiful. The Kraków shoemakers remember Twiner fondly, while the tradeswomen whisper in the market square that a big, green flying dragon still lives on the bank of the Vistula River. The story continues that Twiner collected the remaining bricks and built a new dragon out of them. This one is polite, gentle and kind. He behaves as if he doesn't know what fangs and claws are for! When he meets sheep, he cuddles them and scratches them behind their ears. He spends his days grazing on meadows, and he gets excited when he finds wild strawberries. He puts a garland on his head and wags his lizard's tail when he feels happy. He doesn't breathe fire, but blows rainbow-coloured bubbles instead. He also picks flowers, arranges them in bunches and sings quietly:

Who's the cutest reptile,

In all of Kraków city?

It's the Wawel Dragon,

With a garland that's so pretty!

If you ever hear this song when you stroll by the river, you can be sure that it's him – the smiling dragon that you need never fear.

"Oh dear," thought Aiden to himself. I live in cave, too ... well, a basement flat. I have a green belly. And I can breathe fire like the Wawel Dragon. But perhaps I was rebuilt into a nice dragon with a nervous fire-breathing habit."

A scream interrupted Aiden's thoughts. The sound came from Rita, his neighbour who lived on the second floor.

Aiden immediately rose on his hind legs, spread out his wings, and bared his teeth. A flurry of pigeons flew away. Rita looked in awe at the dragon.

"Are you okay, Rita?" Aiden called up to his neighbour. "Sorry for looking so scary!" He accidentally puffed out another small fire on the grass, which Bob quickly extinguished.

"I'm fine. I just screamed because I caught those pesky pigeons eating my berries again." Rita shook her fist at the pigeons who had moved to a nearby tree. "But you looked amazing, Aiden! And fierce! As fierce as the Wawel Dragon," Rita said.

Aiden's eyes widened. "How do you know about the Wawel Dragon?" Aiden asked.

"It's a famous story where my parents come from," Rita replied. "They used to tell it to me when I was little. I always felt more like the shoemaker than the brave knights."

"Me too," said Aiden.

"But you were very brave just then, when you thought I was in danger," Rita smiled.

Waving towards her potted plants, Rita said, "Like these flowers, we are nice and pleasant most of the time. But we can call on our fierceness when we need to protect something or ourselves."

Aiden thought for a moment. "Do you think the Wawel Dragon was protecting something? Or maybe even himself?"

Rita looked surprised. "I never considered that before. I always thought he was a horrible, scary dragon. But maybe he was protecting something."

"Be right back," Aiden said. When he returned, he had a bunch of bricks and set to work building a bird feeder.

"You're going to feed those pesky birds?" Rita asked.

Aiden put the bird feeder near the tree they lived in, away from Rita's balcony. Then he said, "Maybe the Wawel Dragon was just hungry and needed his own space. With this bird feeder, I hope the pigeons will leave your plants alone now."

"That is very wise," Rita said, inspired by Aiden's kindness. She gave Aiden some strawberries and thanked him for his help.

Settling on the lawn again, Aiden opened his book to the next legend, and read his grandmother's note:

Some stories claim it was dragons who created humans. One such story is the legend of Quetzalcoatl from Mexico. Just like you, Quetzalcoatl was a dragon with many gifts to share.

The Legend
of Quetzalcoatl

By Naibe Reynoso

Before humans existed, there was a powerful Aztec god in Central Mexico named Quetzalcoatl. His body was the shape of a large green serpent, and his head was adorned with bright feathers of emerald green, vibrant red and glowing yellow. He also had the ability to shift into different shapes.

In the ancient language of Nahuatl, "quetzal" means plumed bird and "coatl" means serpent. That is why this dragon is known as the "feathered serpent."

Quetzalcoatl was the god of the sun and the air, the creator of the world and humanity. He was many gods in one, as he was also known as the god of knowledge, art and agriculture. He was strong, majestic and powerful, but he was also lonely.

One day, as he looked upon the empty universe, he decided to create people.

To do this, Quetzalcoatl knew he would have to embark on a difficult journey to the underground world of Mictlán. This journey required him to retrieve the sacred bones of creation. Quetzalcoatl knew this journey would not be easy as he would have to pass through nine layers of the underworld, squeezing through narrow passageways, to reach the bones.

Quetzalcoatl, being so grand and mighty, worried he wouldn't fit.

"Aha!" he said suddenly. "I will just shapeshift into the human shape I wish to create!"

As he prepared for his quest, Quetalzcoatl gathered his cloak and shield for protection.

He also called for his twin brother, Xolotl, a dog-headed god, to travel with him and be his guide.

Their voyage to the underworld was full of challenges. First, they had to cross a large river.

"Hop on my back," said Xolotl. "I will carry you across."

Then, Xolotl walked ahead of Quetzalcoatl, guiding him through many tunnels. After travelling through a cold snowstorm and then climbing over a sharp volcanic mountain, they took a moment to rest. But when it started raining arrows, Quetzalcoatl used his sturdy shield to protect them both.

"Thank you, Quetzalcoatl, you are a kind god," said Xolotl.

The next layer was called Tepeme Monamictlán, which means "place where the mountains meet". It was a big rock wall. Quetzalcoatl used his strength to move some heavy boulders so they could get to the other side.

Finally, Quetzalcoatl and Xolotl reached the last layer of the underworld – the place of the sacred bones! But they still had to get past the powerful Lord Mictlantecuhtli, who guarded the bones.

Xoltol saw a shell on the floor and thought of a plan. "Quetzalcoatl, pick up the shell and blow into it to make loud music," he said. "I will also do something to distract Lord Mictlantecuhtli."

"Great idea," said Quetzalcoatl, and he picked up the shell to do what Xolotl told him.

While Quetzalcoatl blew loud noises from the shell, Xolotl jumped on Lord Mictlantecuhtli and licked his face!

With Lord Mictlantecuhtli distracted, Quetzalcoatl gathered the bones. He quickly took off as Xolotl ran behind him, barely escaping the grasp of Lord Mictlantecuhtli.

"We make a great team!" Xolotl said to Quetzalcoatl.

And from that pile of bones, Quetzalcoatl created the first humans.

Quetzalcoatl wanted the people to be smart, so he gave them things to read and a calendar to keep track of the stars.

They were so grateful that the people built Quetzalcoatl a large temple to thank him for all his gifts.

For a long time, the people were joyful. But after a while they became hungry and sad. They needed better food and more nourishment.

The villagers were nervous of asking Quetzalcoatl for more things. He had already given them so much. Eventually, a brave little girl decided to approach him.

"Quetazalcoatl, we are tired of only eating roots," she said. "The elders speak of a magical food on the other side of the mountain."

Impressed by the little girl's courage, Qutezalcoatl was determined to retrieve this magical food.

"I am glad you spoke up," he told the little girl. "Otherwise, I would have never known what was making you all so sad."

So Quetzalcoatl set out on another journey to travel to Tonacatépetl, the Mountain of Sustenance, and bring this special food back to the people.

The Mountain was very, very tall. Taller than Quetzalcoatl had expected. As he got closer, a giant red ant suddenly appeared and blocked his way.

"Where do you think you are going?" asked the red ant.

"I'm going to collect food from the Mountain of Sustenance," replied Quetzalcoatl.

"That special food is only meant for gods, not humans," said the ant. Suddenly, more red ants appeared to guard the mountain and block Quetzalcoatl from entering.

What was Quetzalcoatl to do? He wanted to avoid conflict, but he needed to get to the other side of the mountain.

"I know!" Quetzalcoatl thought. "I will use my shapeshifting ability to get past these guards."

Poof! Quetzalcoatl turned himself into a tiny black ant and squeezed through the tiny cracks in the mountain, undetected by the red ants. He was overjoyed that his plan had worked.

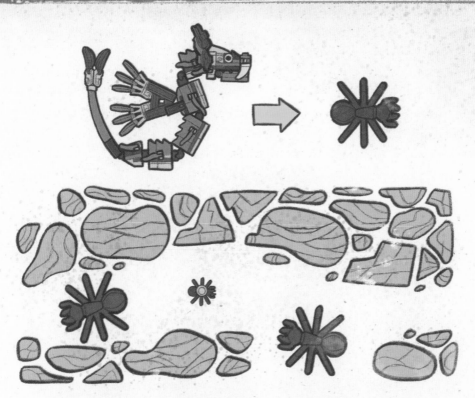

Because he was so tiny, it took him many days to cross the mountain. But he didn't give up. He kept thinking of how brave the little girl was, and he didn't want to let her down.

"She was so courageous, and I need to be, too!" Quetzalcoatl thought.

Finally, after many days, Quetzalcoatl saw piles and piles of corn kernels. From far away, they looked like gold coins, and the food was the best treasure he could find.

Still in ant-form, he took a few kernels on his back, so he could return to the people with this precious new food.

When Quetzalcoatl reached the village, he transformed back into a majestic, feathered serpent.

"Plant the kernels and you will receive precious maize," said Quetzalcoatl. "And with it you will make the most delicious dishes."

From those kernels grew large crops of corn that the people shared to feed everyone. The people also made all sorts of delicious dishes together. Everyone celebrated! Quetzalcoatl felt his time with humankind

was almost complete. But he wanted to leave them with one last gift. What could it be? He decided he would ask the brave little girl what her wish would be.

"You gave us books to read, stars to look at and amazing corn to eat," she said. "How about something sweet?"

Quetzalcoatl was amazed by the little girl's creativity. "You are a brave and smart little girl," he said. "One day you will make a great leader."

Quetzalcoatl then remembered that his brother Xolotl would always eat a specially shaped fruit that he picked from a cacao tree. Quetzalcoatl asked him to pick a few beans to take to the people.

Xolotl refused. "This fruit is for gods, not humans," he said, deciding to stand guard by the cacao tree.

Disappointed, Quetzalcoatl waited until Xolotl fell asleep, and then removed a branch full of bean pods.

"Xolotl won't notice that one little branch is missing," he thought.

Quetzalcoatl raced back to the village before Xolotl awakened to present the people with this sweet present.

"With these cacao seeds you can make chocolate, the delicious drink of the gods," said Quetzalcoatl.

The plant needed a lot of water to grow, so Quetzalcoatl asked Tlaloc, the god of rain, to water it.

Soon enough, everyone was enjoying rich, delicious cocoa. They drank sweet hot chocolate, ate chocolate bars and made other yummy desserts from this most precious bean.

The Earth was now a sweeter place.

This was the last gift Quetzalcoatl gave to his people.

At night, when no one was watching, Quetzalcoatl disappeared into the vast ocean. He was never seen again, but he was never forgotten.

After he left, the villagers realized that although they now had corn to make amazing meals, and delicious chocolate, the best thing that Quetzalcoatl had given them was the gift of sharing. So, from then on, everyone shared their gifts with each other to honour Quetzalcoatl, the generous dragon serpent.

Aiden ate the last of the strawberries. He thought how some dragons like to live alone, but Quetzalcoatl liked living with people. But he wasn't sure what his grandmother meant by the gifts he had to share. He was just regular old Aiden. At least now he knew that his colourful wings were just like Quetzalcoatl's.

He unfurled his beautiful, feathered wings and leaped into the air for a short flight. He didn't normally feel like flying, but the cool breeze whipped across his golden scales, and he lengthened his wings in the most satisfying stretch.

As he landed, he heard his neighbour Tansanee shout, "Bravo, Aiden!"

He looked up at the small figure inside the top floor flat, standing behind a canvas with a paintbrush in her hand. Tansanee was an artist.

"Your scales are making the most marvellous light," Tansanee said. "I started painting you while you were reading, but now I'm painting you flying. I'm running out of canvas!"

She turned her canvas around, and Aiden lifted off again, flapping his wings gently as he hovered in front of Tansanee's balcony. Aiden couldn't help but admire how Tansanee's art seemed to capture a happy feeling.

Tansanee asked Aiden what made him want to fly, as she hadn't seen him do that in such a long time.

Aiden explained that he'd been reading a book that his grandmother had given him. Somehow, the story of Quetzalcoatl had inspired him to stretch his wings.

Tansanee understood. "Making art definitely makes me feel like flying. But I don't have wings like you. Oh, how I wish I had more space to paint you!"

Aiden picked up the white bricks he had left over from building Rita's pigeon feeder. He then flew up and added the white bricks to Tansanee's painting, before launching himself into a spectacular barrel roll.

"Bravo, Aiden!" Tansanee cheered as she furiously painted on to the new blank space. She then said, "Did you know that 'Quetzalcoatl' means 'feathered serpent'? Your name, Aiden, means 'little fire.' A big fire is out of control, dangerous and scary. But a little fire is warm, constant and useful. Like your friendship. It's an extraordinary gift."

Aiden thanked Tansanee and went back down to the grass. He opened his book at the next legend. His grandma had written:

This next legend is about Aido-Hwedo from West Africa. It's a story about being inspired by the friends we choose to be with. Imagine, create, build and enjoy the adventure of living.

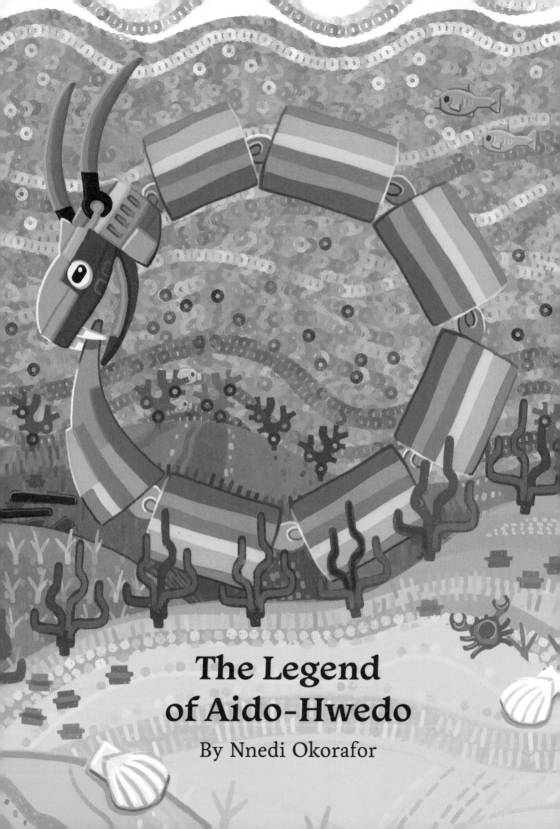

The Legend
of Aido-Hwedo

By Nnedi Okorafor

In the beginning, an adventurous woman in a lovely black, red, white and purple dress wandered alone across a vast savanna wilderness dotted with baobab trees and dusty bushes. There were other people around, but there was no one else like her. Some said she was a witch. Others thought she was a great wisewoman. However, few were brave enough to call her what she actually was: a powerful goddess called Nana Buluku. She was also very lonely. The more she worried about this, the lonelier she felt.

"I want companionship," she muttered to herself as she walked. "But not just any type of companionship. I want someone who measures up to me. Someone who will bring me joy."

Being a goddess has its advantages, for the words she spoke aloud tumbled into the air and took on a life of their own, galloping around the dry, dusty lands to locate her wish. And so it wasn't long before she was led to hear talk of another being who was truly one of a kind. This being's vibrance could light up the world. Immediately, Nana Buluku set out to find this other.

She searched high and low for the marvellous being. Along the way, she had wild adventures that left her feeling lonelier than ever.

One day, she climbed a hill. At the other side of that hill, lying in an oasis of flowers at a drying pond, was the one Nana Buluku had been seeking. It had a massive, serpent-like body that shone in the sun with reflective scales of every colour. When the dragon rolled around in the sunlight, it was as if it gave off colourful stars. By now, she knew its name: Aido-Hwedo, the rainbow serpent.

Nana Buluku introduced herself and, for a while, Aido-Hwedo only looked at her through narrow eyes of distrust. Nana Buluku was annoyed at first. Then she considered the fact that maybe Aido-Hwedo was also lonely and in need of companionship. So she swallowed her pride and told the dragon of her travels and the wildest of her adventures. Still, Aido-Hwedo remained unimpressed. It was only when Nana Buluku spoke of her loneliness and need for someone who was like her that she caught Aido-Hwedo's attention.

"You are truly interested in me for who I am?" Aido-Hwedo asked.

"Yes," Nana Buluku laughed. "I have lived long and seen much. You are marvellous."

Aido-Hwedo opened its gigantic mouth, the inside glowing electric blue with lightning, and roared a sound like wind and rain. Its breath smelled of wet grass and thunder as it rushed over to Nana Buluku, blowing her braids back and wetting her face with rainwater. And just like that, it was as if Nana Buluku understood Aido-Hwedo's history. Aido-Hwedo had gone on many amazing adventures, too, even travelling into the cosmos to taste the colours of foreign planets and stars. Then it had returned to Earth out of loneliness, for no place was like Earth and it was sure it would find a worthy companion here. Alas, it had been a very long time and Aido-Hwedo had still not found a friend.

"We are so much alike," Nana Buluku said.

Aido-Hwedo agreed, delighted. "Let us build together," it said. "I have many ideas, and you inspire even more in my mind."

"We will bring joy and fun to the community!"

"My thoughts exactly," Aido-Hwedo said.

The two new friends talked well into the night. Nana Buluku had many ideas, and Aido-Hwedo loved them all. When the sun rose, they began to build. It was a celebration. They built mountains, wove complex jungles, laid out vast fields, grew and sprinkled plentiful soil. They transformed everything around them. Aido-Hwedo wriggled and writhed its giant serpent body to create new valleys, graceful hills, winding rivers and deep, sharp canyons. In the evenings, it flew through the heavens, breathing fire and creating stars and lightning bolts.

The two got so carried away with creating, they forgot to balance it all out. They had built so much that now they feared their amazing world would tip over and collapse!

To make things worse, having worked so hard to create the abundant new world, Aido-Hwedo's body was boiling hot, utterly overheated from all its activity. The lightning and fire that naturally lived within it was churning and crashing, for great joy is still a type of energy. Nana Buluku feared that Aido-Hwedo's fires would get out of control and ruin their creations.

"Come," Nana Buluku said. And she led Aido-Hwedo to one of their freshly created oceans. "Cool off in here."

Aido-Hwedo dove into the cool, salty waters, swimming into the depths. At first the waters boiled around the serpent, but as it went deeper, the temperature became more stable. Aido-Hwedo reached the bottom of the ocean where it coiled all the way around the Earth in a giant loop. Then it clamped its tail in its mouth. And here, calmed and cooled, Aido-Hwedo settled and rested. Clever undersea monkeys swam up to the serpent, curious and delighted to have such an interesting visitor in their midst. Aido-Hwedo's body warmed their waters to a comfortable temperature and, in turn, when it grew hungry, they brought it their iron rods they had mined and forged themselves.

Aido-Hwedo stayed here for a while, comfortable and content. Sometimes, after eating too many of the delicious iron rods, there would be bolts of lightning bouncing wildly in its belly and it would have to shift around to calm them. Its movement would shake the lands and waters, causing great earthquakes and tsunamis. Even the monkeys had a hard time with this, as the shaking waters destroyed whole neighbourhoods and even swallowed one of their iron mines.

Everyone far and wide ran to take cover from Aido-Hwedo's stomachaches. After some time, people sought out and asked Nana Buluku if she could convince Aido-Hwedo to come back from the ocean floor. Nana Buluku was happy to help, as she missed her friend dearly. Nana Buluku came up with the plans for building vast watering holes around the world and the people of the land built them, creating lakes!

Then, Nana Buluku searched a river and found a giant, light-blue sapphire that was shaped like a ball and sparkled like galaxies. She giggled with excitement as she sat in a boat and held it over the water. Aido-Hwedo loved sparkly things and Nana Buluku knew it wouldn't be able to resist the sapphire, even from the depths of the ocean. Sure enough, Aido-Hwedo came up to see the great stone. When the dragon saw Nana Buluku, it no longer wanted to be in the deep. It had missed her, too.

Nana Buluku led Aido-Hwedo to the new bodies of water that had been built, and her friend was even more amazed. It excitedly dove from lake to lake and Nana Buluku followed, laughing at its glee as the waves tossed her boat about. As Aido-Hwedo bounced from one lake to the next, it would playfully show off for Nana Buluku, spraying a long trail of water droplets.

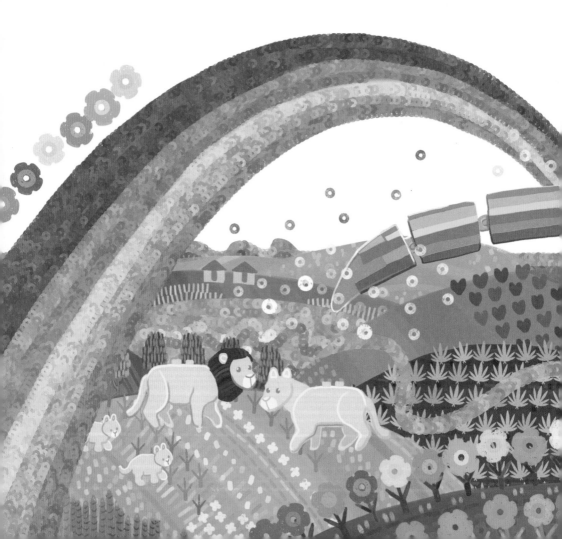

These droplets rained down from the sky and provided water for people, other animals, plants and crops. The playfulness of Aido-Hwedo and Nana Buluku made Earth more fertile than ever! And there was a bonus. In the wake of these water trails came colourful spectacles of light: rainbows!

To this day, people from around the world recognize rainbows as a sign of the joy, beauty, creativity, friendship, balance, harmony and diversity found in all life, landscape and nature. Friendship can truly be a magical thing, especially when friends build together.

Aiden finished the last legend and felt a deep connection to his roots. He couldn't remember if he had arrived at Long Meadow before Ben, Rita and Tansanee, but it didn't really matter. The important thing was that he lived in a beautiful home with friends who liked him for who he was and appreciated his differences. After all, being different is special.

Aiden looked around Long Meadow, taking in the view. Bob had finished washing his windows and was now starting on Rita's windows, but he lost his balance on the top step.

"WHOAAA!" Bob wobbled. Aiden quickly collected some leftover bricks and steadied the ladder.

Aiden was feeling brave now, and asked Bob to hold out his metal bucket. Aiden relaxed his shoulders and took a deep breath. He then puffed out just enough fire to heat the water in Bob's bucket.

"Thank you, Aiden!" Bob's eyes lit up. "Not a happy accident any more, but a happy intention."

Aiden flew up again to Tansanee's flat and asked if he could borrow some paints.

"Of course!" Tansanee said, handing them over, then clapping her hands with excitement. "Keep them as long as you like, but I would really like to see what you paint."

Aiden promised he would share when he was finished. That gave Aiden another idea, and he asked Rita if she could bring some strawberries over to his flat tomorrow.

"I'd much rather you ate them than those thieves!" Rita said, still eyeing the pigeons on the bird feeder.

Aiden thanked Rita and then tucked his book under his wing, collected his leftover bricks and went back inside his home.

When he looked in the mirror this time, Aiden started to feel like he wasn't a mess at all, but a dragon with a purpose, just like his amazing ancestors. He had colourful wings like Quetzalcoatl. A serpent-like face like Aido-Hwedo. A fiery breath like the Wawel Dragon. And a golden tail like Yinglong.

Inspired by Tansanee, Aiden decided to make his own picture, partly from real life and partly from his imagination.

First, Aiden used his bricks to build a blank canvas. Sitting in front of the mirror, he painted what he saw: parts of Yinglong, the Wawel Dragon,

Quetzalcoatl and Aido-Hwedo. Stopping for a cocoa break, Aiden's tail caught the leg of the easel.

WHACK!

Aiden accidentally spilled his mug of cocoa.

SPLASH!

His canvas crashed to the ground.

SMASH!

Aiden landed on top of it.

He looked at his ruined work and felt defeated. He had been inspired by the dragon legends and almost convinced himself that he could be the same as the heroes of those stories. Maybe he was nothing like them after all.

But then Aiden thought of his wonderful grandmother, who always saw the best in him. Then he thought of Bob, Rita and Tansanee, and how they had seen his gifts. And then he had a new idea.

He set Tansanee's paints aside and started building. Brick by brick, a new picture began to take shape. Just like the shoemaker in the Wawel Dragon legend, perhaps he could rebuild his art into something better.

The next day, Aiden looked at his artwork and decided it was finished. He carefully covered it with a soft cloth to keep it hidden until his big unveiling.

Aiden called to his neighbours, inviting them to see what he'd made. Rita grabbed her basket

of strawberries, and with Bob and Tansanee, they trundled down to Aiden's basement flat.

Aiden greeted them each with a mug of cocoa, and they all shared Rita's strawberries. The dragon removed the cloth to reveal his artwork: a mosaic showing him with his grandma, and symbols of the legendary dragons above them.

Bob, Rita and Tansanee all ooh-ed and aah-ed.

"I don't know if the dragon legends in my book are real or not," said Aiden, "but what are real are my friendships with you. You all inspired me to create this. Thank you!"

"You can see the family resemblance," said Rita.

Bob added, "You must be very proud to come from a long line of legendary dragons."

Tansanee said, "And we are so proud to have you as our neighbour and friend."